THE ORIGIN OF SUPER K

BY

KYLE J WILLIAMS

For permissions and other inquiries, please contact:

Josh0279@hotmail.com

ISBN: 9798865840329

First Edition: 2023

This book is dedicated to all the superhero fans who dream of seeing their characters conceived in their minds come to life.

Contents

Chapter One

THIS IS HOW IT ALL BEGAN

To everyone else, it was just another normal day in Kayville but not for Kyle. The day started as normal, but little did he know that this day would change everything.

“Ding Ding Ding!”, went Kyle’s alarm clock.

“Oh no, is it that time already?” Kyle yawned and rubbed his eyes. As Kyle looked over the side of his bed, he could see his alarm clock shaking up and down as it went off. It was 7:00am, Monday morning and time to get ready for school. As he rose from his bed, he slowly approached his window to draw back his curtains to peek outside.

The birds were singing their happy songs whilst the wind danced to their rhythm. The magnificent, majestic sun shone in the crystal-clear blue sky. The occasional lily-white clouds passed through the air, as if saying “hello,” to all the birds in the sky. The tallest skyscrapers, offices, factories, and houses were spread out throughout the city. People greeted each other as they took their time to get to work, or hurriedly barged past each other to get to their destination.

“Kyle, Kyle”, said Kyle’s mum quietly, as she peered into his room. “Come on Kyle, time to get into the shower, you’re going to be late.”

“Yes mum.” As Kyle got up, he wondered what the day had in store for him. It was Monday, P.E. day and football after school. He would get to see his friends and couldn’t wait for breaktime.

After Kyle got ready, he went downstairs for breakfast. “Eat up Kyle, we haven’t got long before we’ve got to go. Make sure your bag is packed, and when you’re finished, grab your coat from under the stairs”.

“Yes mum”.

As Kyle went to grab his coat, something seemed different, there was a light coming from under the stairs, but he hadn’t turned the light on. The light was so bright, a golden, glossy colour. It was like when the sun shone on the lemon sand at the beach. Kyle could hear a strange noise coming from underneath the staircase, like what he had heard from the trains whizzing by at Lumber Jack Station.

As he got closer, Kyle felt nervous and excited at the same time. A heavy wind caught Kyle off guard, swinging the door open and…

VOOM! he was sucked into the light, with the door shutting behind him.

“Weeeeeeeeeeeeeeeeeeeeee, yeahhhhh”, it felt like a rollercoaster at a super awesome theme park, speeding through the air, flashing lights all round. “What is happening, where am I, how did this happen?”. So many questions, but with a bump, Kyle came to a stop. “Wow, this is cool, but where am I”?

As he looked around, Kyle felt different, he wasn’t hurt but he felt stronger, faster, and lighter, yes lighter! Kyle jumped into the air but didn’t come down. “I can fly, I can fly”!

“Hello young man, I’m glad you are here, it’s very nice to meet you but please don’t stare”.

“Who said that? Where are you? show yourself! I am Kyle, please come out, what is your name?”

“Hello young Kyle, my name is Ragon the Dragon. I will come out but don’t be scared, I’m not very tall as my height has been impaired.”

From behind a tree emerged Ragon the Dragon. Ragon was a rare and endearing creature. known everywhere in the land of Fableton, Ragon was known for his unique charm and small appearance. Unlike the towering dragons of legends, Ragon stood at about three feet tall, making him one of the most approachable and beloved beings in all Fableton.

Ragon had soft, emerald-green scales that sparkled in the sunlight, with patches of vibrant sky-blue ones that shimmered like sapphires. His round, button-like eyes twinkled with an inviting warmth, each one a brilliant shade of golden-yellow. His small-scaled wings, resembling those of a delicate butterfly, were adorned with intricate patterns of colours that change when you look at them from different angles, and patterns that glowed when he was excited. Ragon's tail was short and curled, and it sported a fluffy puff of blue-coloured fur at the end.

One of Ragon's most enchanting features was his expressive face. His wide, toothy grin was always brimming with joy and mischief, and his eyes sparkled with curiosity. When he was excited, his eyes would light up like twinkling stars in the night sky, and his tail would wiggle with delight.

Ragon was known for his boundless enthusiasm and his ability to rhyme when he spoke. Despite his small stature, Ragon possessed a strong sense of determination, never letting obstacles keep him from his goals.

Chapter Two

RAGON'S RELIABLE RESEARCH

"I am Ragon, and I have come to help you on your quest."

"What quest?" asked Kyle, "One minute I was at home getting ready for school, and the next minute I am here with what seems to be superpowers!"

Ragon explained to Kyle that the reason he was there was because he is the chosen one. Ragon explained the Great War to him and what Kyle's part was. The Great War was the biggest war known to man. It all began when a former hero, Super Laser, had enough of fighting for good and justice, so he betrayed all superheroes and became the villain known as Dark Laser. Dark Laser, together with Mr Time (another villain) created a villain society to defeat all superheroes. Ragon explained that he had been searching both time and space for a suitable person with the qualities of a superhero to protect Fableton and ultimately to become the protector of Superhero City.

Kyle was the final piece of the puzzle. He would protect Superhero City till the end of time, and would be named, Super K.

Kyle, now with his newfound identity of Super K, agreed. With an eagerness to take on this new challenge, he listened intently on what needed to be done.

"First, you need to find Mr time and defeat him. He will likely be in his headquarters. I would suggest that is the first place you should go, but you must also understand what you are up against. Mr. Time is a villain who can manipulate time itself. Covered in mystery, he is an enemy as complex as the very fabric of time. He can bend it to his will. His appearance is a captivating blend of timeless composure and charm, making him a formidable adversary for any superhero daring to confront him."

Standing at a magnificent six feet tall, Mr. Time had a lean and imposing figure that exuded an aura of power and leadership. His body seemed to be flowing with an otherworldly energy, giving the impression that he was not entirely bound by the laws of physics like ordinary mortals. His skin was unnaturally pale and scary to look at.

He donned a tailored, ebony black suit that seemed to absorb and reflect light in peculiar ways, causing it to shimmer. His crisp white shirt and perfectly knotted blood-red tie added an eerie contrast. Over his suit, he wore a long, sweeping black coat that billowed dramatically as he moved, giving the impression of an interdimensional presence.

Perhaps the most striking feature of Mr. Time was his fake face, engraved with the deep lines of age and wisdom. His eyes were pools of infinite darkness, inky orbs that held secrets of time's endless depths. His salt-and-pepper hair, slicked back with precision, hinted at his wisdom and experience.

Around his neck, Mr. Time wore a pendant in the shape of a golden hourglass, an emblem of his control over time itself. The sand within the hourglass flowed and ebbed at his command, symbolizing his control over the passage of moments. He also sported a pair of gloves, each adorned with a complex web of interlocking gears, a visual representation of his temporal powers.

Mr. Time had an intellect that rivalled the greatest minds in history. He was forceful and well-spoken, his words flowing with a charm that could attract even the most steadfast heroes to listen to his devious plans.

His concluding goal was a rule over ultimate power and control, a drive driven by his belief that time itself should bow before him. He looked to reshape history and alter the course of events to serve his jaw gaping desires, believing that he alone held the key to unlocking the secrets of eternity.

In the world of heroes and villains, Mr. Time stood out as a formidable foe who could twist the very essence of existence itself. His complex character and mastery over time made him a figure of both fascination and fear, a challenge that Super K would face with braveness and determination.

Chapter Three

THE MASTER OF TIME

Super K’s journey to find Mr Time began with a thunderous clap of lightning. As Super K soared through the night sky, his red cape billowed in the fierce wind, like a comet's tail. His super-senses tingled with anticipation as he contemplated the challenge ahead of him.

As he descended into the mystical Forest of Whispers, the ancient trees whispered secrets to him. Super K could hear the leaves rustle in excitement, as they shared tales of Mr. Time's misdeeds. The forest was alive with weird creatures – wise owls with feathers as white as the moon, mischievous animals who hid behind mushrooms, and trees that sparkled with fairy lights. Super K had to use his keen intellect to navigate through this magical maze.

In the heart of the forest, he met the Riddle Sphinx, a magnificent creature with the body of a lion and the wings of an eagle. The Sphinx blocked his path and declared,

"To defeat Mr. Time, answer my three riddles. Only then shall you pass."

Super K, always up for a challenge, accepted it.

I have keys but cannot open locks. I have space but no room. You can enter, but you cannot go inside. What am I?

“A keyboard!” shouted Super K.

Correct. I am taken from a mine and shut up in a wooden case from which I am never released, and yet I am used by almost every person. What am I?

This one was trickier. Super K stood for a moment, trying to think what this could be. He could not possibly fail before he had even started, but then with a flash of inspiration, as if a light bulb was turned on, it came to him,

“A pencil, lead, graphite”!

Yes, well done. Lastly, I am not alive, but I can grow; I do not have lungs, but I need air; I don't have a mouth, but water kills me. What am I?

I know this one. A fire!!

The Sphinx's riddles were cunning and cryptic, filled with metaphors and hidden meanings, but with his quick thinking, Super K solved each one, and the Sphinx, in awe of his wisdom, allowed him to pass.

As Super K continued his journey, this was not the only challenge he would face, there was more in store that he would need to overcome. Ahead, Super K spotted what looked like a vast body of water, it was in fact the treacherous Sea of Shadows, where the waves whispered secrets of ancient shipwrecks and pirate legends. The sea was as dark as the darkest of nights, and the animals that roamed it were as dull as Kyle when he had to do maths homework!

The sea roared with tempestuous rage and the relentless waves crashed against spikes that towered above Super K.

Super K, determined to cross, used his power of creation to build a shimmering bridge of light that guided him safely to the other side.

On the distant shore, he met the Mermaid Oracle, a mysterious being who sang songs of prophecy. She revealed a cryptic vision of Mr. Time's hideout, an island hidden in the mists of the Timeless Sea. Super K thanked the Mermaid Oracle and headed to the Timeless Sea, flying for what seemed like miles. As he arrived, he remembered what the Mermaid Oracle had shown him. He would need to dive into the depths of the Timeless Sea, using the sound of ticking clocks, echoing, in the watery depths, as his guide to the underwater Timeless Island.

Finally, he reached the Timeless Island, a place where past, present, and future all became one deadly mess. Mr. Time's lair was a towering clock tower, which stretched out of the ocean-bed, high into the ocean, far from prying eyes. In the tower, each face of a clock displaying a different era stretched for miles up the tower. Super K ascended the tower, dodging hourglass traps and spinning gears, until he reached the top.

Chapter Four

TIME'S UP!

Mr. Time, a sinister figure cloaked in shadows, surrounded by swirling clocks, stood in the shadows. As Super K approached him, without any hesitation, Mr Time attacked.

The battle that ensued was a spectacle of dazzling time-bending powers and heroic antics by Super K.

Firing clocked shaped weapons towards Super K which, if they landed on Super K, would transport him to a different era. Mr Time was sure that he would destroy Super K and never let him reach Dark Laser. Super K retaliated with laser eyes to destroy each clock that was thrown at him.

Mr Time decided to up his game, and using an extra special clock, the wheel of time, he opened time vortexes to every possible death Super K could encounter across different dimensions. Super K tried everything, but nothing could destroy the wheel of time. Suddenly, Super K thought of an idea. He darted from wall to wall evading each deathly clock, until he found an object he could throw into the wheel of time. Everything he found and threw into the clock shut another vortex until there were no more left.

Mr Time was frustrated, so he decided to find a time where he was in control and had thousands of soldiers to destroy Super K. With that, Mr Time created a portal to travel to the year 4023, where Super K was dead, and Mr Time has taken control of the entire universe. Super K darted towards the portal to destroy it, but Mr Time used his time blast to send Super K backwards.

In a final burst of energy, Super K used his quick thinking to summon an almighty burst of lightning to fire at the portal, destroying it.

In a final plan to destroy Super K, Mr Time attempted to alter the timeline to a time when Super K was not the chosen one and where Mr Time and Dark Laser ruled over the world.

Unfortunately for Mr Time, when Super K shut down the portal, that also shut off Mr Time's powers, making him powerless. In a moment of victory, Super K sent Mr Time into the depths of the ocean, hoping to trap him long enough to defeat Dark Laser.

With Mr. Time defeated and the flow of time restored, Super K returned to Ragon as a hero; knowing full well that he may have won this battle, but the war had just begun.

Chapter Five

DARK LASER'S DRAMATIC ENTRANCE

As the victorious Super K shared a delightful chat with the powerful Ragon, Super K wondered why Dark Laser wanted to assume control of the world, and why he attacked it in the first place.

"I can sense that you want to hear the origin of the dictator Dark Laser. Am I right? Very well."

"It all truly began when I banished Dark Laser and Mr Time to Supervillain City. They had been concealed in the barrier of my powers for what seemed like an eternity. In the course of time, Dark Laser and Mr Time manufactured a plan to destroy the barriers of reality and travel through the different dimensions. First, they needed a way out of the prison and into the city. They brainstormed for what seemed like decades, until Dark Laser realised that if he combined his powers with Mr Time, the combination of endless power would be strong enough to break free from their captivity. Knowing that combining their powers would mean that he may never get back to full strength, it was worth the risk to escape. He ordered Mr Time to turn the wheels of time and keep it open long enough for him to begin his plan.

As Ragon continued speaking about the nefarious Dark Laser, the sun lowered, and the bird's happy songs started to end as they dwindled in numbers. In a sudden change of mood, Ragon's voice started to lower and suddenly, it became a dark sinister voice.

"As Mr Time opened the time vortex, I used my dark energy and powered through the time ball and altered the past, knocking Ragon down with my dark matter, allowing my past self to escape and find a new location to plot my master plan to destroy…"

"What!" exclaimed Super K, interrupting Ragon in mid speech.

Abruptly, a dark force lifted up Ragon and spun him up in the air. A black and purple cape clicked round his neck, as a red and black glowing logo appeared on his chest. Donning a Red and Black suit and hovering in front of the defensive Super K, the once calm, affectionate and most humble resident of Fableton City turned into the malevolent, corrupt, wrathful, and destructive Dark Laser!

"Didn't expect that now, did you Super K?"

"What have you done with Ragon the Dragon?"

“Ragon will just be taking an eternal nap for now”, bellowed Dark Laser as he laughed cunningly. When you were fighting Mr Time, I snuck into Fableton and transformed myself into Ragon. I used my power to put him in a sleep that he will never wake up from, without the use of this waking powder.”

Dark Laser pulled out a small container filled with light blue powder, waking powder. Waking powder was the only substance that can wake Ragon from the eternal sleep, imposed on him by Dark Laser.

“I will stop you!” Yelled Super K.

“You, stop me? Ha!! you are no threat to my grand plan. Since your faithful Ragon is no threat to me anymore, Superhero City is the one place left to conquer, making the residents my faithful slave subjects. Until we meet again Super K!”

With that Dark Laser was gone. Super K stood there confused. How would he stop Dark Laser he wondered, where was Ragon? How could he save Ragon and Superhero City? Feeling powerless, Super K stood there in shock, unable to believe what had just happened. Dark Laser had outwitted him, and now he was free to conquer Superhero City. No one knew about the forthcoming attack, and to make matters worse, today was the 45th anniversary of Superhero City. Super K knew that he had to do something, but he did not know what. He was feeling confused and powerless.

Chapter Six

THE RIDDLE TO SAVE RAGON

Suddenly, he knew he had to snap out of it, focus and find Ragon. Ragon was the only one who could help him stop Dark Laser. But where was he? Super K had to find him, and fast. He quickly scanned the area, but Ragon was nowhere to be seen. Taking to the sky, Super K flew as fast as he could, searching all areas, looking for any clue as to where Ragon was being held.

Just then, in the distance, Super K spotted something that did not look quite right. Dark Laser's forces had surrounded a cave, they were guarding something, could it be, it must be where Ragon is being held. Super K knew that he had to rescue Ragon, but he did not know how. He was outnumbered and outmatched by Dark Laser's forces, but he had to try. He owed it to Ragon.

He took a deep breath and charged into battle. He fought bravely, but he was no match for the vast number of Dark Laser's minions. He was beaten and bruised, and he knew that he could not defeat them on his own.

Just when it seemed like all hope was lost, a familiar voice rang out.

"Super K!"

Super K looked up and saw Riddle Sphinx standing there, his eyes blazing with anger.

“Riddle Sphinx!" Super K cried. "What are you doing here!"

"I saw what happened to Ragon whilst you were gone, I was powerless on my own to stop Dark Laser. Now you are back I'm not going to let Dark Laser’s forces take you down without a fight, you must come with me first to train, trying to save Ragon alone will surely lead to your defeat."

Super K left with Riddle Sphinx, with the knowledge of what needed to be done. Together with Riddle Sphinx, Super K trained for weeks, getting stronger and stronger. He learned new fighting techniques and developed new strategies. He was ready to rescue Ragon.

Super K headed back to where Ragon was being held with Riddle Sphinx by his side. They had a plan; Riddle Sphinx would attempt to distract Dark Laser's forces with Riddles, whilst Super K creeped in to rescue Ragon. As Riddle Sphinx approached the cave, he was at once met with hostility and weapons drawn by Dark Laser's forces.

"Stop! What are you doing here! You have no business here Riddle Sphinx. Yes, we know who you are."

"What has roots as nobody sees, is taller than trees, up, up it goes, and yet never grows?"

"What?" exclaimed Dark Laser's forces.

"No, not What, A mountain!" said Riddle Sphinx.

"I have eyes but cannot see, I have ears but cannot hear, I have a mouth but cannot speak, what am I?"

"We have no time for your Riddles, Riddle Sphinx, be gone or we will make you disappear."

"Wrong again" said Riddle Sphinx, "the answer you were looking for is A book".

"That's It!"

Dark Laser's forces left their post and charged towards Riddle Sphinx. As quick as a cheetah, Riddle Sphinx spun around and began to run. As they chased Riddle Sphinx, the plan was working, Riddle Sphinx had done enough to cause a distraction to allow Super K to sneak into the cave to begin the rescue mission.

Super K, aware that Dark Laser's forces were cunning and may not be gone for long, he knew he needed to be quick but also needed a plan B. By carefully studying Dark Laser's forces whilst Riddle Sphinx was distracting them, Super K disguised himself as one of those useless minions. In the distance he could see two minions coming towards him, he needed to remain calm, but how could he, he would be surrounded if he were caught. As the minions came closer and the fear began to slip in, would the disguise be enough, his heart felt like it was beating as loud as a drum,

"Evening".

"Evening!" replied Super K as he walked past them, it had worked! The disguise had held up, this was his chance.

"Umm, I was told to move the prisoner, remind me, which cell is he being held in again? That Riddle Sphinx is out there causing trouble."

"The prisoner is being held in the last cell on the right." We will deal with that Riddle Sphinx!"

Super K raced to the cell where Ragon was being held, hoping not to be spotted.

As he arrived, there on the floor, behind the thick metal bars was Ragon. Super K quickly looked around, confident no one was coming, he used his super strength to bend back the cell bars and enter the cell.

“Ragon, Ragon!” Called Super K, but there was no response. Ragon was still under the curse of eternal sleep, regardless of this, Super K knew he needed to get Ragon out of there to somewhere safe. He picked up Ragon, holding him as tight as he could, he left the cell. With a loud thunderclap, he flew straight out of the cave, leaving the minions in his dust, wondering what had just happened.

It was time to get to Superhero City to put a stop to Dark Laser and get the waking powder to wake up Ragon. Before Super K could get to Superhero City, he knew there was one being he needed to see again, Riddle Sphinx.

“Tell me about Superhero City,” asked Super K, “I must go to save Ragon and save the city”.

Riddle Sphinx explained that Superhero City is a place where dreams come true. It is a place where anything is possible, Where the good would always triumph over evil, and where everyone is welcome. It is a beacon of hope in a dark world, a place where people can come together to make a difference. However, with Dark Laser there, all this will be in jeopardy. Head towards the tallest mountain, flying as fast as you can. A vortex will open as you hit the speed of light, and through that, you will get to Superhero City.

With Ragon on his back, Super K left Riddle Sphinx, arriving in Superhero City in what seemed to be no time at all.

Chapter Seven

SUPERHERO CITY TAKE-OVER

The sun hung low on the horizon, casting long shadows across the cityscape. Super K's red cape fluttered gracefully behind him as he touched down on the rooftop of a tall tower. He needed somewhere to leave Ragon whilst he continued his quest, and this seemed like the perfect place. Ragon was unconscious, but he was breathing.

Super K was on a quest. A quest to find Dark Laser, a cunning and elusive villain who had been wreaking havoc across Superhero City. Dark Laser's crime spree had risen, and it was clear that his sinister plan was reaching its climax.

Super K took a deep breath and looked around. The city was quiet, but he knew that Dark Laser was out there, somewhere. He had to find him, and he had to stop him.

Super K started to walk, his cape flowing in the light wind behind him. He did not know where he was going, but he knew that he had to keep moving. He had to find Dark Laser, no matter what it took.

He walked for hours, until he came to a dark alleyway. He hesitated for a moment, but then he stepped inside. The alleyway was deserted, but Super K could feel a presence there. A dark, evil presence was lurking somewhere close. Super K took a deep breath and walked deeper into the alleyway. He knew that he was getting closer to Dark Laser. He could feel it in his bones.

The streets were deserted, this did not seem like the Superhero City Riddle Sphinx had described, it was clear that Dark Laser's evil plans had taken shape.

As Super K came to the end of the alleyway, there, standing in the shadows, was Dark Laser. His eyes were red, and they burned with hatred.

"So," Dark Laser said. "You've finally come to face me, Super K."

"I have," Super K said. "And I'm going to stop you."

"You think you can stop me?" Dark Laser laughed. "You're nothing but an insect to me."

Super K's jaw clenched, his determination burning brighter than ever. "We'll see about that," said Super K.

Super K squared his shoulders, his resolve unwavering.

With a sudden burst of speed, Dark Laser lunged forward, his form a blur of energy. Bolts of shadowy energy shot from his hands, crackling through the air toward Super K. But Super K was ready, his reflexes honed to perfection, those weeks of training with Riddle Sphinx had not been in vain. With a swift motion, he raised his shimmering red cape, deflecting the dark projectiles with a resounding clang.

The alleyway became a battleground, a canvas for their clash of power. Super K soared into the air, his cape billowing dramatically, and unleashed a torrent of brilliant energy beams that lanced toward Dark Laser. Dark Laser retaliated, conjuring a swirling vortex of darkness that threatened to consume everything in its path.

Chapter Eight

THE BATTLE BETWEEN GOOD AND EVIL

As energy collided with shadows, the very ground trembled beneath them. The echoes of their battle reverberated through the vast skies, alerting the citizens to the epic confrontation unfolding in their midst.

Super K and Dark Laser clashed like titans, their powers pushing each other to the edge. The alleyway was bathed in a tornado of colours, a dazzling display of light and darkness, as their forces met with explosive fury.

Super K knew that he carried the hopes of Superhero City on his shoulders, and he was ready to face any challenge. With every ounce of strength and resolve, he pushed forward, determined to bring an end to Dark Laser's reign of terror, and to prove that, in the end, justice would always triumph over hatred.

The battle was fierce, and both Super K and Dark Laser were injured. Super K battled Dark Laser like there was no tomorrow. With bolts of energy being thrown, and punches being delivered, Super K discovered new powers that he did not even know he possessed, such as: Laser eyes, super strength, invisibility, teleportation and many more still waiting to be unlocked. The Battle raged on for hours, both fighters using all their strength to overpower the other. Super K and Dark Laser almost managed to knock each other to their end, but they were both too powerful to be defeated by simple strategies.

Eventually, Super K managed to knock Dark Laser off his feet and have him at his mercy.

“It is over Dark Laser. You have lost. Give up.”

“NEVER!”

Dark Laser zoomed up into what seemed like an everlasting sapphire Sky, which soon turned into a dark space that seemed like it was made from a strange substance, like Dark Matter. Super K used his super flight to catch up with Dark Laser in space. With both in an area where they could unleash their true power, Super K did not hold back.

Super K clenched his fist until it turned a light golden colour, he used the power to upper cut Dark Laser into a flowing asteroid.

CRASH!

As Dark Laser collided with the asteroid, he came plummeting back down. Super K used his laser eyes to shoot Dark Laser further in the everlasting space. Dark Laser was dazed, and shocked by Super K's power and was ready to give it his all.

Dark Laser charged at Super K ready to deliver his most powerful blow but, as he flew towards Super K, Super K began to glow. The exact same glow that he saw under his stairs. He felt powerful, indestructible. It was always meant to be.

As Dark Laser charged towards him, his face turned from vengeance, to dumbstruck. Super K spread out his arms, looked further up into the sky, and his eyes glowed. Super K knew what was happening, he let out a massive burst of energy, which flung Dark Laser backwards. Super K knew that he had now acquired the powers of the First Golden Master.

In the never-ending battle between good and evil, the first Golden Master once ruled over the good and evil, until the forces of evil decided to rise-up and fight back. The battle raged on for centuries, and only ended when the leader of those possessed with evil, destroyed the First Golden Master, sending him into an ever-lasting vortex.

Dark Laser was not ready to give up yet. He also powered up and became a figure that the residents of the world would recognise. Dark Laser was the evil that destroyed the first Golden Master. He was the ultimate evil that was said to return. The battle now did not just hold the fate of Superhero City, it now held the weight of the entire universe.

Chapter 9

UNTOLD POWER

Super K and Dark Laser began a battle that would set the stage for all great battles in the future. With powerful energy beams being shot by both of them, blasts of good and evil spread throughout space, until Dark Laser unleashed something deathly. In a shockwave of energy, Dark Laser fired a radio wave of energy at Super K.

Super K returned the energy with his own flow of energy at Dark Laser. This was the true final battle, good vs evil.

Super K and Dark Laser each used their powers, and in a flash of Golden light, Dark Laser came crashing down to the ground, with Super K zooming down behind him.

Dark Laser crashed into the ground, as he did, that dark shadow lifted over Superhero City, returning it to its former glory.

“Give me the waking powder, now!” shouted Super K.

Dark Laser reached into the depths of his pocket and pulled out his blue waking powder. As quick as lightning, Super K snatched the powder and flew back to where Ragon was.

Flicking the lid off, he poured the powder over Ragon and if by magic he woke up.

"Ragon, can you hear me?"

"Yes, thank you Super K, I and the city will forever be in your debt."

Super K smiled. He was glad that he had been able to save his friend. Super K helped Ragon to his feet, and together, they walked away from the scene and Super K transported Ragon back to his home and left him to rest, while Super K continued his journey to protect the universe and his new home, Superhero City.

Super K was hailed as a hero, and he vowed to always protect the city from evil. He knew that Dark Laser would be back, but he was confident that he would be ready for him.

THE END

Super K will return in, Super K: A New Foe

Printed in Great Britain
by Amazon